Abi Cushman

WOMBATS ARE PRETTY WEIRD

A [not so] serious guide

GREENWILLOW BOOKS

An Imprint of HarperCollinsPublishers

Meet the wombat.

Excuse me?
I'm a snake.

The wombat is a robust,

        sometimes elusive . . .

. . . burrowing marsupial.

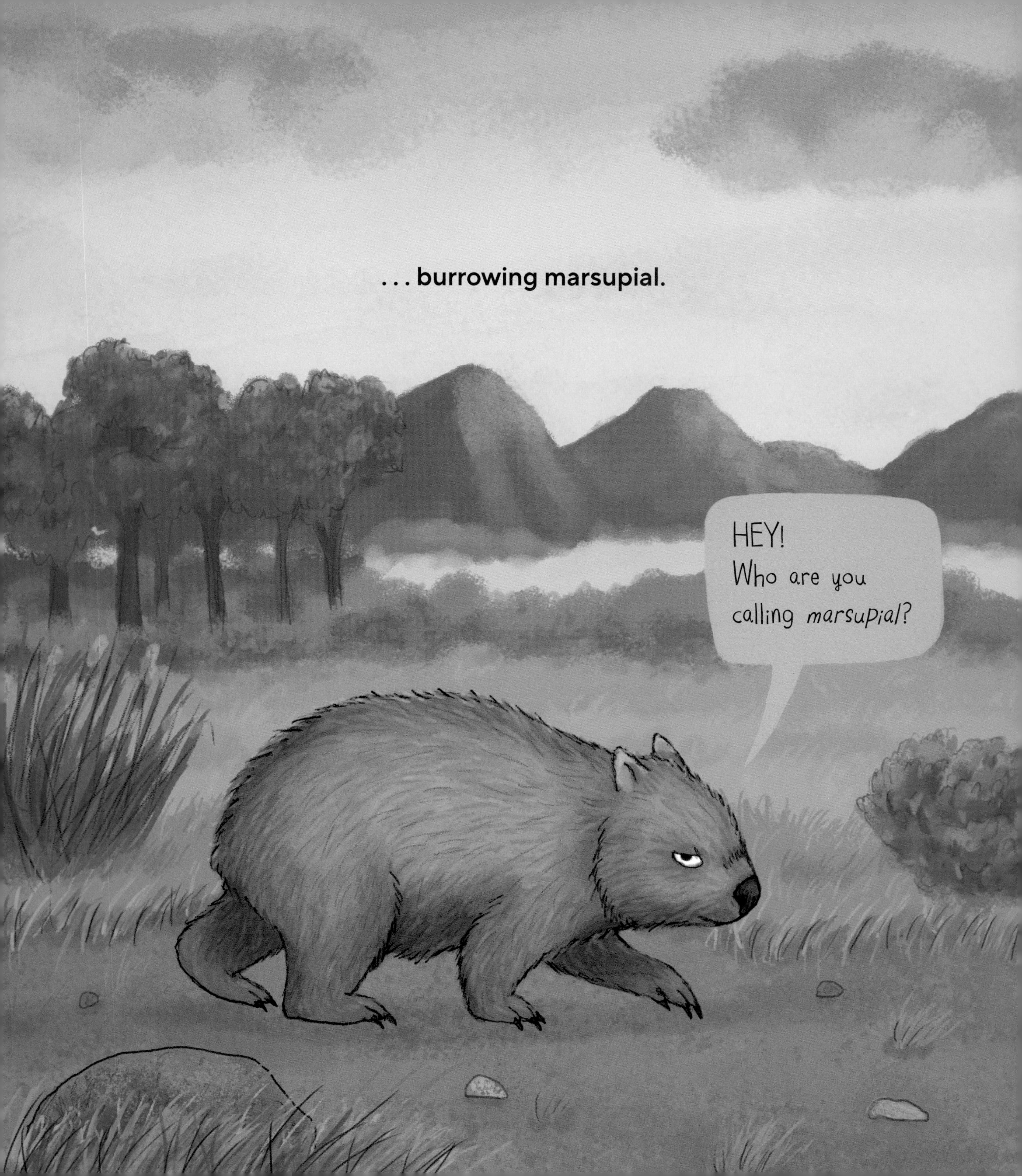

Marsupi–WHAT?

A marsupial is a type of mammal that generally carries its young in a pouch (a pocket-like fold of skin on the mother's belly).

Other examples of marsupials are koalas, kangaroos, wallabies, Tasmanian devils, quokkas, and numbats.

YEAH!
And who are you calling *elusive*?
I'm right here!

Oh. Not me?
Never mind, then.

Did you take the picture yet?

My arm's not long enough!

CHEEEEESE!

Wombats live in the shrublands,

forests,

and mountains of Australia.

Wombats are nocturnal and can walk as far as 2.5 miles in one night.

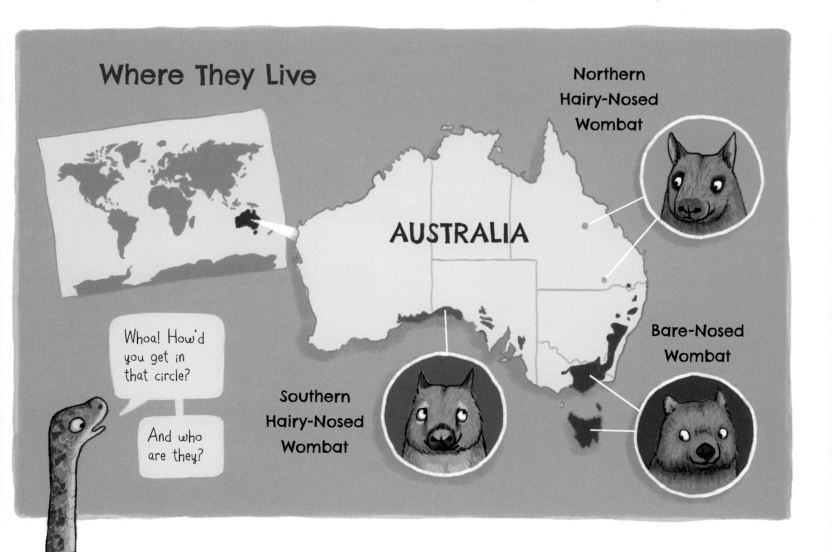

There are three species of wombat.
Two of the species have hair on their noses.

Southern
Hairy-Nosed
Wombat

Northern
Hairy-Nosed
Wombat

One does not.

Bare-Nosed
Wombat

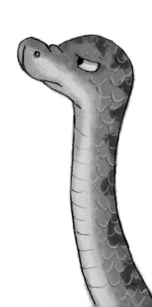

These names
seem a little . . .
on the nose,
if you ask me.

Baby wombats are born blind, hairless, and the size of a jelly bean. But they manage to climb all the way into their mother's pouch without any help.

Pouch Potato

For the first six to seven months of its life, a baby wombat stays in its mother's pouch and does nothing but drink milk, sleep, poop, pee, and grow.

Wombats have backward-facing pouches. Unlike a wallaby or kangaroo pouch, a mother wombat's pouch opens up toward her rump, not toward her head. This helps keep dirt out of the pouch when the mom wombat (or "mombat," as we like to say) is digging.

Backward pouches?

I'm telling you, Joanne, rear-facing pouches are so easy to keep clean. You really should give them a try.

No dirt in here! Just an old jelly bean—hey, we're the same size!— a spare key, and a tiny mitten.

Like all baby marsupials,
baby wombats are called joeys.

A wombat's teeth never stop growing.

NEVER?

Yup. That's right. NEVER.

In fact, they are growing
RIGHT
NOW.

Which means . . .

. . . wombats can eat tough vegetation like grasses, sedges, bark, moss, and roots every day without grinding their teeth all the way down to nubs.

And they can gnaw through non-food items too. Like fences.
(They do this a lot!)

You know . . . there's a gate right over here.

Oh, don't worry. My teeth will be fine! They never stop growing, you know.

munch!
munch!
munch!

Unlike any other animal in the world, wombats have cube-shaped poop. They leave piles of their flat-sided feces on the ground and on top of logs and rocks to mark their territory. One wombat might drop as many as one hundred cubes in a single night.

The Scoop on Cube Poop

How is cube poop formed when no part of a wombat's digestive tract is shaped like a square?

Here's what we know: It takes two to four days for food to travel from a wombat's stomach through its tube-shaped intestines and out of its body as droppings.

The poop starts out very mushy and not cube-shaped, but it becomes harder and drier as it moves through the intestine and moisture is pulled out.

Nothing square back there, thank you very much!

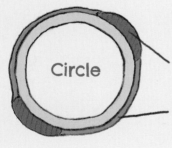

Wet & Mushy → Dry with Corners → Cracked into Hard Cubes

The cube formation happens toward the end. In the last part of the intestine, there are four bands of muscles that run along its length. Two of the bands are thinner and stretchier, and two are thicker and stiffer.

When the intestine contracts (or squeezes), these bands mold corners into the poop and create a square shape.

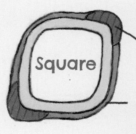

Intestine Relaxed

Circle

Thick, stiff muscle band

Thin, stretchy muscle band

Intestine Contracted

Square

Thick, stiff muscle band squeezes corner

Thin, stretchy muscle band bows out to form corner

As the wombat absorbs moisture from the intestine, the square poop hardens and breaks into droppings. Since the droppings are so hard and dry by the end, they keep their cubic shape as they exit the body.

Wombats are tough. Literally. They have thick fur, and their butts are armored with a layer of cartilage. Cartilage is the strong, flexible tissue also found in your nose and ears.

When confronted by predators (like dingoes, foxes, or Tasmanian devils), wombats run into their burrows and use their sturdy backsides to block the entrance.

You know, you could just add some kind of door.

Oh, no need! I'll just keep using my butt. It's made of cartilage, you know.

Wombats spend most of their time underground. They usually have several burrows, which can range in size from a simple three-foot-long tunnel to an extensive network of tunnels and chambers spanning as far as one hundred feet.

My other burrows are more spacious, but you just can't beat the views in this one.

Though wombats may share their burrows with other wombats (and sometimes other animals, like rabbits, lizards, foxes, and wallabies), they are generally solitary animals, and spend most of their time alone.

Is now a good time to tell you that I sent out a bunch of party invitations?

Wombat bodies are built for burrowing. They have short, muscular legs, and long, flat claws, which are ideal for digging tunnels.

Tunnels!

But NOT ideal for making balloon animals.

POP!

Even though wombats
may be terrible balloon artists,

I asked for a poodle.

Err . . . how
about just a
snake this time?

YEAH!
SNAKE!

WOM-BAT!
WOM-BAT!

there are no other animals quite like these
burrowing, cube-pooping marsupials.

And that makes wombats pretty weird . . .
but also pretty wonderful at the same time.

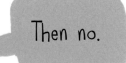

Then no.

Southern Hairy-Nosed Wombat

Scientific Name: *Lasiorhinus latifrons*

Length: 30–36 inches

Weight: 42–70 pounds

Conservation Status: Near Threatened

Threats: Sarcoptic mange
(a skin disease caused by mites), drought, and habitat loss

Southern Hairy-Nosed Wombat

Northern Hairy-Nosed Wombat

Wow! I am *really* photogenic, don't you think?

Northern Hairy-Nosed Wombat

Scientific Name: *Lasiorhinus krefftii*

Length: 39–45 inches

Weight: 70–88 pounds

Conservation Status: Critically Endangered, with small
populations in two protected areas in Queensland, Australia

Threats: Loss of habitat and native grasses, predation by
dingoes, and drought

Bare-Nosed, or Common, Wombat

Bare-Nosed, or Common, Wombat

Scientific Name: *Vombatus ursinus*

Length: 33–45 inches

Weight: 48–86 pounds

Conservation Status: Least Concern

Threats: Sarcoptic mange
(a skin disease caused by mites)

What's a gloss-ar-ree?

Glossary

Burrow: A hole or a tunnel that an animal uses as a home.

Cartilage: Strong, flexible tissue that can be found in your ear, your joints, or in a wombat's butt.

Contraction: The process of squeezing or getting smaller.

Digestion: The process of breaking down food into smaller parts that can be absorbed by the body.

Glossary: A list of words and their meanings.

Intestine: A tube, connected to the stomach, that food travels through.

Marsupial: A type of mammal that carries its young in a pouch.

Nocturnal: Being active at night.

Pouch: A pocket-like fold of skin located on a female marsupial's belly.

Sedge: A grasslike plant.

Shrubland: An area of land covered in shrubs, small trees, and grasses.

Further Reading

"About northern hairy-nosed wombats." Queensland Government; Brisbane, Queensland, Australia. Accessed January 2, 2022. https://www.qld.gov.au/environment/plants-animals/conservation/threatened-wildlife/threatened-species/featured-projects/northern-hairy-nosed-wombat/

Divljan, Anja. "Bare-nosed Wombat." Australian Museum. Accessed January 2, 2022. https://australian.museum/learn/animals/mammals/bare-nosed-wombat/

Gamillo, Elizabeth. "Wombats Poop Cubes, and Scientists Finally Got to the Bottom of It." *Smithsonian Magazine,* February 8, 2021. Accessed January 2, 2022. https://www.smithsonianmag.com/smart-news/scientists-have-solved-mystery-how-wombats-poop-cubes-180976898/

Berry, Ruth, dir. NOVA. Season 49, episode 2, "Secrets in the Scat." Aired February 9, 2022 on PBS. https://www.pbs.org/video/secrets-in-the-scat-5xekub/

Triggs, Barbara, ed. *Wombats.* Clayton: CSIRO Publishing, 2009.

"Wombat *Vombatus ursinus, Lasiorhinus krefftii, Lasiorhinus latifrons.*" San Diego Zoo Wildlife Alliance. Accessed January 2, 2022. https://animals.sandiegozoo.org/animals/wombat

Yang, Patricia J., Alexander B. Lee, Miles Chan, et al. "Intestines of non-uniform stiffness mold the corners of wombat feces." *Soft Matter,* 2021, 17: 475-488. https://doi.org/10.1039/D0SM01230K

Acknowledgments

A special thank-you to Dr. Scott Carver, lecturer in wildlife ecology at the University of Tasmania, for helping me get all my cube poop facts straight. And to Graham Lee, a volunteer at Epping Forest National Park in Queensland, Australia, for providing a photo of the very elusive northern hairy-nosed wombat. And to Andy Podolsky, wombat conservation advocate, for all his assistance.

Can You Find These Other Australian Animals?

 Bandicoot

 **Dingo**

 Kangaroo

 Koala

 **Numbat**

 **Possum**

 Quokka

 Quoll

 Tasmanian Devil

 Wallaby

For my joeys, Scout and Finn

Wombats Are Pretty Weird: A (Not So) Serious Guide
Copyright © 2023 by Abi Cushman

All rights reserved. Manufactured in Italy.
For information address HarperCollins Children's Books,
a division of HarperCollins Publishers, 195 Broadway, New York, NY 10007.
www.harpercollinschildrens.com

The full-color artwork was drawn in pencil and colored digitally.
The text type is 16-point TT Norms Pro.

Library of Congress Cataloging-in-Publication Data

Names: Cushman, Abi, author, illustrator.
Title: Wombats are pretty weird / written and illustrated by Abi Cushman.
Description: First edition. | New York, NY : Greenwillow Books, an Imprint of HarperCollins Publishers,
[2023] | Includes bibliographical references. | Audience: Ages 4–8 | Audience: Grades 2–3 | Summary:
"Wombats are elusive, burrowing marsupials. Their teeth never stop growing, they have backwards
pouches, and they're the only known animal to have cube-shaped poop. And if you ask their snake
friend, those aren't the only things that are weird about wombats!"— Provided by publisher.
Identifiers: LCCN 2022036362 | ISBN 9780063234437 (hardcover)
Subjects: LCSH: Wombats—Juvenile literature.
Classification: LCC QL737.M39 C87 2023 | DDC 599.2/4—dc23/eng/20220819
LC record available at https://lccn.loc.gov/2022036362

23 24 25 26 27 RTLO 10 9 8 7 6 5 4 3 2 1
First Edition

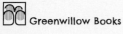 Greenwillow Books

Look! I'm in a circle, too!

Joey the snake